UNBEARABLY GROSS

What is John Wayne Bobbitt's favorite flick?

Return of the Magnificent Seven.

———

Why can't lepers get a drivers' licenses?

They always leave their feet on the gas.

———

Why can't Ted Kennedy give blood?

They can't get all the cocktail olives through the tubes.

———

How can you tell when a Hell's Angel is happy?

He's got bugs in his teeth.

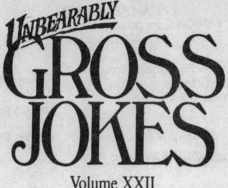

UNBEARABLY GROSS JOKES

Volume XXII

by Julius Alvin

ZEBRA BOOKS
KENSINGTON PUBLISHING CORP.

ZEBRA BOOKS are published by

Kensington Publishing Corp.
850 Third Avenue
New York, NY 10022

First Printing: March, 1996
10 9 8 7 6 5 4 3 2 1

Printed in the United States of America

CONTENTS

GROSS ETHNIC JOKES

Why are Jewish men like linoleum?

Lay them right and you can walk all over them for the next thirty years.

———

A black, a Jew, and a redneck are walking along the beach. One of them kicks a bottle and a genie pops out.

The genie says to the trio, "Whoever kicked the bottle and released me is entitled to three wishes."

Neither the black, the Jew, nor the redneck can remember which one of them actually kicked the bottle, so the genie says, "Then I will grant you each one wish."

The black guy goes first. He says, "I want all the African-Americans to go back to Africa and live free of oppression!"

"So shall it be done," the genie promises, and snaps his fingers. The black guy disappears.

The Jew goes next. "I want all the Jewish people to go to Israel and live free of oppression."

"So shall it be done," the genie says and snaps his fingers. Poof, the Jew disappears.

The genie turns to the redneck, "And what is your wish?"

"Now let me get this straight," the redneck says. "You sent all the blacks back to Africa and all the Jews back to Israel?"

The genie nods.

"Then hell," the redneck declares. "I'll just have me a beer!"

Why did the Polack buy a Spanish-American dictionary when his third son was born?

Because he read that every third person born in America is Hispanic.

What do they say about Martin Luther King Day in Alabama?

"Kill four more and we'll take the whole week off."

———

How does a Mexican know when he's hungry?

His asshole stops burning.

———

Why aren't there any black skydivers?

Because their lips explode at 20,000 feet.

Why did the Polack go to the pet cemetery?

He wanted to visit his childhood sweetheart.

———

What do you get when you cross an Italian and a Polack?

A hitman who keeps missing.

———

What's the difference between a black guy and a pothole?

You swerve to *avoid* a pothole.

A truck driver is hauling a load of bowling balls through the deep south. He sees a black guy hitchhiking by the side of the road, and stops to pick him up.

"Got no room in the cab," the trucker says to the black guy, "but you're welcome to sit back there with the bowling balls."

The black guy does.

Ten miles up the road, the trucker sees a second black guy hitching. The trucker stops and makes him the same offer. The second black guy climbs into the back with the bowling balls and the first black guy.

Ten more miles up the road, the trucker sees a little black boy hitchhiking. The black boy has a bicycle with him, though it has two flat tires. The trucker picks him up as well. He goes into the back of the truck with the two black guys and the bowling balls.

Driving through a small Mississippi town, the trucker is pulled over for speeding by two state troopers. While the first one is writing out the ticket, the second trooper decides to see what kind of load the trucker is carrying. He opens the back door and sees the three black guys and the bowling balls.

The second trooper rushes back to the first and says, "Tear up that ticket, Orville, and get this truck out of town now!"

"Why?" the first trooper asks.

" 'Cause this truck's carryin' two niggers and a shitload of nigger eggs. Shoot, one of them's already hatched and stole hisself a bicycle!"

What do you call a black man who uses condoms?

A humanitarian.

A Polish woman goes to the doctor. "Doctor, I've been using that diaphragm like you said, but I think it's making me sick."

"What seems to be the problem?" the doctor asks.

"Every time I use it," the Polish woman says, "I have this terrible purple discharge."

"Are you using the jelly with the diaphragm like I instructed?" the doctor wants to know.

The Polish woman nodded. "What kind of jelly are you using?" he asks her.

"Welch's Grape," she replies.

What do you call three black guys sitting in a garden?

Fertilizer.

What's the definition of a nigger?

An African-American who just left the room.

Ninety-year-old Epstein is on his deathbed. He calls for the rabbi.

"Rabbi," Epstein says to him, "I'm going fast. I want you should convert me to Christianity."

"But why?" the doctor asks, quite shocked at Epstein's request.

"Because if somebody has to die," Epstein replies, "let it be one of those bastards!"

Why was the Polack late for his own wedding?

He couldn't find a clean bowling shirt.

Why do white people throw their garbage away in clear plastic bags?

So Mexicans can go window shopping.

Hear about the Million Man March in Washington, D.C.?

Four guys missed work.

What's the name of the movie Hollywood is making about the Million Man March?

A-pack-of-lips Now

What do grapes and noses have in common?

Mexicans like to pick them both.

———

What's the definition of a Greek gentleman?

A guy who takes a girl out on at least three dates before he propositions her little brother.

———

What do you get when you cross a Chinese woman and a black woman?

Someone who'll suck your shirts.

What do you call a French restaurant that serves soul food?

Chez-*what?*

What's the last thing an Irish politician runs for?

Mexico.

An 87-year-old man goes to confession.

"Bless me, Father, for I have sinned," the old duffer says.

"What is your confession?" the priest asks.

The old man says, "I cheated on my wife of sixty years with a fifteen-year-old girl," the old man says.

The priest is horrified. He says, "That's terrible. Tell me, I don't recognize your voice. Have you come to me before?"

"No," says the old man. "This is my first confession. Truth is, Father, I'm Jewish."

"Let me get this straight," the priest says. "You cheated on your wife with a fifteen-year-old girl and you're Jewish. Why are you telling me this?"

"Hell," the old man says. "I'm telling everybody!"

A Polish woman goes to her doctor. Her knees are covered with bruises.

"Those bruises are awful," the doctor says. "How did you get them?"

The Polish woman replies, "Well, doctor, we make love . . . sort of . . . well, doggie style."

"I see," the doctor says. "I think you'd better try a different position until those bruises go away."

"Oh, but we couldn't," the Polish woman exclaims. "My dog's breath is murder!"

———

Two black guys meet on the street.

"Where you been lately?" the first black guy asks his friend.

"I got married," the second black guy replies.

"That's great," says the first. "How's the sex?"

"Not great, announces the second black guy. "But at least I don't have to wait on line."

How do you break an Irishman's index finger?

Kick him in the ass.

What did Hitler say when Mussolini dropped by unannounced?

"If I'd known you were coming, I would have baked you a kike."

Two Polacks are flying from New York to Chicago. Suddenly the pilot makes an announcement over the intercom. "We seem to have lost power in one engine, but there's nothing to worry about, except that we're going to be 45 minutes late."

Ten minutes later, the pilot is back on the intercom. "Ladies and gentlemen," he says, "we seem to have lost power in a second engine, so it looks like we're going to be two hours late."

Twenty minutes later, the pilot comes on again and sounds very nervous. "Ladies and gentlemen, we just lost the third engine, so we're going to be three hours late."

"Shit." one Polack says to the other. "We lose that fourth engine, and we'll be up here all day!"

What's the difference between a Jewish woman and an Italian woman?

The Italian girl has real orgasms and phony diamonds.

What do an alcoholic and a pub in Belfast have in common?

They both get bombed.

What's an Irish seven-course meal?

A sixpack and a boiled potatoe.

How do you brainwash a Polack?

Give him an enema.

Why are there so many virgins in Ireland?

Because all the pricks are in the United States.

What are the first words out of a Jewish boy's mouth?

"You want to cut off the end of my what?"

What's black and red and can't get through a revolving door?

A nigger with a knife in his back.

Hear about the Jewish terrorists who hijacked a plane?

They ransomed it for ten million dollars in pledges.

Hear about the Polish terrorists?

They staged a raid on the Special Olympics.

Why did the black kid hide in the freezer when he got diarrhea?

He thought he was melting.

———

Why do black folks keep chickens in their yards?

To teach their children how to walk.

———

What's the definition of an accountant?

A Jewish boy who can't stand the sight of blood.

Why did the Polish hemophiliac die so young?

He went to an acupuncturist.

What's a Jewish threesome?

Two headaches and a hard-on.

Why did the Polish girl wear red lipstick on her twat?

Because red meant STOP—WRONG HOLE.

How do you know a Korean has just robbed your house?

The cat is gone and your homework is done.

Why do blacks like hats with wide brims?

To keep the birdshit off their lips.

Hear about Ku Klux Knievel?

He jumped over ten niggers with a steamroller.

What's black and brown and looks good on a nigger?

A doberman.

What's a black teenager's best subject in school?

Addiction and subtraction.

What's the first question they ask you in a Mexican restaurant?

Shooting or non-shooting section?

Why do black men love eating pussy?

They smell like catfish on the outside and look like watermelon on the inside.

A black guy checks into a motel with his best friend's wife. He signs the register with a big X, then draws a box around it.

"I've seen a lot of folks sign in here using an X," the clerk says, "but why did you draw a box around it?"

"Sometimes a guy doesn't like to use his real name," the black guy replied.

———

A Polack takes a trip out to the country and visits an orchard where you can pick your own apples.

The Polack asks the owner, "How much?"

The owner says, "All you can pick for five dollars."

The Polack hands the farmer a bill and says, "Fine. Give me ten dollars' worth."

———

Why did the Polack bring a ladder to the party?

He heard that drinks were on the house.

MORE GROSS ETHNIC JOKES

Why does it take nineteen Polish men to go to a porno movie?

Because the sign said, "Under Eighteen Not Admitted."

———

Why did the Irishman stuff tin foil up his nose?

He wanted to keep his dinner warm.

What do Polish women wear under their arms?

Odor-Eaters.

What's a Haitian's favorite song?

"Sit Down You're Rocking the Boat."

What was the black kid's favorite book?

The Cat in the Hat Be Back

How do teachers take attendance in Bosnia?

With a show of hands.

What do you call an Ethiopian with feathers up his ass?

A dart.

What does a Jewish American Princess say right before she has an orgasm?

"I need to hang up now, Mom."

Why was the Jewish mother buried at Bloomingdales?

So her daughter would come visit twice a week.

What do you call sex with a black man?

Rape.

What do they use for birth control in Nicaragua?

Contra-ceptives.

How did the Mexican die during the pie-eating contest?

The cow stepped on his head.

What do Koreans call the dogcatcher's wagon?

Meals on Wheels.

What's a Korean's favorite meal?

Muttloaf.

Why can't Italians become Jehovah's Witnesses?

Because they don't like witnesses.

Why do black men know exactly when they're going to die?

Because the warden tells them.

What do you call an Arab herding sheep?

A pimp.

How many Italians does it take to screw in a lightbulb?

Three. One to screw it in, one to be a witness, and the third to shoot the witness.

———

How do you know when a kid is half-Jewish and half-Italian?

When he goes to confession, he brings a lawyer.

———

Why was the Polish baby black and blue?

His mother burped him with a sledge hammer.

What do you call a Jewish pig?

Roseanne Bar-Mitzvah.

What do you call a Jewish racist?

Ku Klux Klein.

Why did the Jewish vampire die?

He tried to get blood from a stone.

What's a Mafioso's favorite meal?

Broken leg of lamb.

Sammy, an old Jewish man, is walking along Miami Beach. He sees an old bottle. He picks it up and rubs it a few times, and a genie pops out.

The genie says, "I will grant you two wishes for freeing me from the bottle."

Sammy says, "Only two wishes? Most genies give three."

The genie responds, "Hey, this is the nineties. We got inflation. You only get two wishes."

"Fine," Sammy says. He pulls out a map of the Middle East and shows it to the genie. "So here is a map of Israel and the rest of the Middle East. The Arabs want to destroy Israel and my people. I want you should grant me my wish and make peace throughout the Middle East."

The genie responds, "That's a pretty tall order. Peace in the Middle East? That's downright impossible. What's your second wish?"

Sammy says, "I want that when I come home, my wife rips my clothes off, throws me down on the bed, and makes passionate love to me."

The genie replies, "Let's take another look at the Middle East map . . ."

What do you call a mole on an Italian's ass?

A brain tumor.

What do you call a hundred Mexicans in a Volkswagen?

A family reunion.

Why don't Italians eat fleas?

Because they can't get the fleas' little legs apart.

How many Polacks does it take to screw in a lightbulb?

Two. One to screw it in, one to screw it up.

The Polish guy laments to his friend, "My dog is pregnant. I can't tell you how upset I am."

"How upset are you?" his friend asks.

"I'm so upset," the Polack says, "I just asked the dog to marry me."

What happens when a Polack gets Alzheimer's Disease?

He gets smarter.

What's the first thing a black woman says after sex?

"Next!"

What's the difference between a Jewish American Princess and Jello?

Jello moves when you eat it.

———

Why do JAPS like using Tampons?

Because nothing goes in without the strings attached.

GROSS CELEBRITY JOKES

Who was Susan Smith's driving teacher?

Ted Kennedy.

What is Susan Smith's favorite TV show?

"Sea Hunt."

What killed Jerry Garcia?

Acid indigestion.

Hear about the new limo service O.J. is starting?

They'll get you to the airport with an hour to kill.

———

Why is O.J. moving to Alabama?

The DNA is all the same.

———

What's black, sixty-years old, and is sitting in O.J.'s jacuzzi?

Juror Number Seven.

———

Why can't Ted Kennedy give blood?

They can't get all the cocktail olives through the tubes.

Why isn't Washington's Birthday celebrated in Washington D.C.?

Because a man who can't tell a lie isn't worth remembering.

This gal is so hot for Tom Cruise and Brad Pitt that she decides to have their likenesses tattooed on her butt, one on each cheek. Her boyfriend was furious but wanted to see what they look like.

The girl drops her jeans and sticks out her ass.

Her boyfriend says, "They don't look anything like Tom Cruise or Brad Pitt."

They argued, and the girl said she wanted a second opinion. When the mailman came to the door, she proudly displayed her new tattooed cheeks and asked him, "Do you know whose faces these are?"

"No," the mailman says, "but the one in the middle looks just like Willie Nelson."

How much does Johnny Cochran charge to screw in a lightbulb?

How much you got?

Why won't Louis Farrakhan run for president?

They don't make bulletproof Cadillacs.

What do you call a big fat actress?

Moby Roseanne.

How did Moby Roseanne commit suicide?

She shot herself with a harpoon.

Why are Michael Jackson's pants so short?

They belong to a ten-year-old.

———

What's Michael Jackson's favorite drink?

Seven and Up.

———

What is John Wayne Bobbitt's favorite flick?

Return of the Magnificent Seven.

———

What did the telephone operator say to John Wayne Bobbitt?

"Sorry, but you've been cut off."

What did Jeffrey Dahmer say to Lorena Bobbitt?

"I like mustard on mine."

Why was Lorena Bobbitt arrested?

She got caught littering.

Why is John Wayne Bobbitt like a snowstorm?

They both have six inches on the ground.

What's O.J.'s best golf move?

A slice.

What were David Koresh's last words?

"Getting kinda hot in here, ain't it?"

What's a Branch Davidian's favorite dessert?

Toasted marshmellows.

What's 25-years-old and gets very little sleep at night?

Paula Barbieri.

What weighs 300 pounds and cares about the environment?

Sidney Greenpeace.

What did God say when he created Minister Louis Farrakhan?

"Holy shit!"

What do Roseanne and a hollowed out pumpkin have in common?

They're both heads with nothing inside.

What did Jerry Garcia say to Elvis when he got to Heaven?

"You're not gonna believe who your daughter just married!"

GROSS SEX JOKES

What did the flasher say to his victim during a blizzard?

"It's too cold. Mind if I just describe myself?"

What's the definition of "68?"

You do me and I'll owe you one.

A 99-year-old man calls his lawyer.

"Jake," the old man says, "I need you to come down to the 23rd Precinct and bail me out. I'm in jail."

The lawyer is amazed. The old man is a model citizen.

"What are you in jail for?" the lawyer asks.

The old man replies, "I'm being held on charges of raping a woman."

"This is terrible," the lawyer says. "Did you do it?"

"No," the old man responds.

"Then why are you in jail?" the lawyer wants to know.

The old man says, "I was so flattered, I pleaded guilty!"

———

How do you stop a dog from humping your leg?

Give him a blowjob.

A guy comes home from work one day to find his girlfriend packing her bags.

"What are you doing, honey?" he says to her.

"Alvin, I'm leaving you," she tells him.

"But why?" he asks. "Everything was going so well."

The girlfriend replies, "I'm leaving you because you're a pedophile!"

"Pedophile?" Alvin snorts. "That's a pretty big word for a seven-year-old!"

Why aren't lawyers breast-fed as babies?

Because their own mothers don't trust them.

How do you drown a blonde?

Tell her not to swallow.

What do you call a hooker who services sadists?

Someone who's strapped for cash.

What do you call a doctor who treats only fat women's pussies?

A rhino-cologist.

What do you call an all-nude soap opera?

"Genital Hospital."

A ten-year-old boy is dragged into court on a paternity suit. He hires the best lawyer in town.

At the hearing, the lawyer asks the young boy to stand up and unzip his fly before the judge. The lawyer reaches inside the boys pants and pulls out his tiny, limp dick.

"Your honor," the lawyer begins, wagging the kid's doodle, "take a good look at this small, undeveloped penis. Is it possible that he could father a child with this?"

The lawyer continues on, wagging the kid's dick, until the kid mutters to the lawyer, "You better quit shaking it real soon or we're gonna blow this case!"

What's the definition of a sadist?

A proctologist who keeps his thermometer in the freezer.

What's the definition of sex?

One of the most beautiful, natural, and wholesome things that money can buy.

———

What's the difference between men and women when it comes to sex?

Women need a reason to have sex, men only need a place.

———

What is "34½"?

"69" for midgets.

Little Red Riding Hood is prancing through the forest. The big bad wolf jumps out from behind a tree and cries, "I'm going to eat you!"

Little Red Riding Hood says, "Eat, eat, eat! Doesn't anyone fuck anymore?"

What do you call a magician who likes to squeeze tits?

David Coppa-feel.

What do you call a sex club in Disneyworld?

Pluto's Retreat.

What's the best thing about sex education?

The oral exams.

Why did the Jew buy an artificial vagina in a sex shop?

He heard there was no sales tax on food items.

What's the definition of artificial insemination?

A technical knock-up.

Why did the dwarf get kicked out of the nudist colony?

He kept getting in everyone's hair.

A fifteen-year-old girl asks her father, "Daddy, can I borrow the car?"

Her father replies, "Yes, but only if you give me a blowjob."

The girl is repulsed, but she really wants to use the car. She agrees. Her father drops his pants and shoves his daughter's head down on his cock.

The girls starts sucking, then spits in disgust and cries, "Geez, Daddy, your cock tastes just like shit!"

"Oh, that's right," her father remembers. "Your brother asked to borrow the car an hour ago."

———

What did the elephant say to the guy with a ten-inch dick?

"Very nice, but can you eat peanuts with it?"

What's white and rains down from the heavens?

The coming of the Lord.

On their honeymoon, the couple made love. Afterwards, the bride punched her husband in the nose.

"What's that for?" the husband asked.

His new wife said, "That's for being a lousy lover!"

With this, the husband punched his wife in the nose.

"What's that for?" she asked.

"For knowing the difference!" the husband said.

What do peacocks have sex with?

Peacunts.

How does a deaf woman masturbate?

She reads her own lips.

———

What's the definition of a slut?

A girl who has to get tight before she gets loose.

———

What do you call a dozen vibrators?

Toys for Twats.

———

Herman's wife tells him to be home by six sharp or else. She's tired of him staying out late every night, bowling with his friends.

Herman's secretary, Alice, is a real knockout. At ten to six she says to Herman, "Could you drive me home?"

Her apartment, Herman remembers, is at least ten minutes out of his way. But being a good boss, he agrees, though he knows his wife will be mad. As they're driving to her place, they pass the supermarket.

Alice wants to stop and pick up just a couple of items, won't take a minute. Reluctantly, Herman agrees. Twenty minutes later, they pull up in front of Alice's apartment building. Herman is already half an hour late. Alice invites him upstairs—for just one drink, she claims. Herman can't think of any way out of it, so he agrees—just one drink.

Alice makes them a drink. Then another. Then another. Before long, Herman and his secretary are in bed, fucking their brains out. Hours later, he wakes up and looks at the clock. It's four in the morning.

"Oh, my God," Herman cries. "My wife is going to kill me. I was supposed to be home by six!"

Then Herman gets a great idea. He pours baby powder over his hands, lots of it.

He dressed and rushes on home. He is immediately confronted by his wife, who is very angry.

"And just where the hell have you been?" she asks.

Herman replies, "I gave my secretary a ride home, she invited me up for a drink, and we ended up in bed together."

Herman's wife notices the baby powder on her husband's hands and says, "Don't lie to me, Herman. You were out bowling all night!"

"Yes, honey," Herman says. "I was."

Why do elephants have four feet?

Because two feet won't satisfy a lady elephant.

What's the definition of a rubber?

"Around the cock protection."

What did the whore get when she slept with the judge?

An honorable discharge.

GROSS REDNECK JOKES

What's the shortest book ever published?

The Redneck's Guide to Culture

Why do men from Alabama have sex with their sisters?

Because it's all relative.

How do you circumcise a redneck?

Kick his sister in the chin.

Ten Reasons Why A Beer is Better Than a Woman:

1. You can pick up a beer in any bar in town.

2. You can have more than one beer a night and not feel guilty.

3. A beer doesn't get jealous when you come home with another beer on your breath.

4. A beer never complains about your beer belly.

5. A beer doesn't mind when you bring home another beer.

6. You don't have to wine and dine a beer.

7. A beer doesn't yell when you come home at two in the morning.

8. You don't have to buy a beer flowers.

9. You don't have to clean your underpants for a beer.

10. Hangovers are only temporary.

What has eight legs and two teeth?

A family of four going to the Alabama State Fair.

———

What does a weather report sound like in Alabama?

"A tornado ripped through town and caused six million dollars worth of improvements."

———

What does a redneck call his pick-up truck?

The bridal suite.

What's the definition of a southern gentleman?

A redneck with $200 in the bank.

Two rednecks meet at the local Seven-Eleven.

"How's married life?" asks the first redneck.

"Ain't half bad," replies his friend. "Except when my second wife starts trying to give orders to my thirteen-year-old daughter from my first marriage."

"What's wrong with that?" asks the first redneck.

"My second wife is only twelve."

Two rednecks meet at the local bar. The first one says, "Where you been keepin' yourself Jim Bob?"

Jim Bob says, "Been hanging out at the whorehouse."

"Having fun?" the first redneck wants to know.

"Nope," Jim Bob says. "Been visitin' my kinfolk."

A redneck has sex with his sister. Afterwards, she says, "You fuck a lot better than Daddy does."

"I should," her brother says. "Mommy taught me how."

SIMPLY GROSS

"Mommy! Mommy!" the little boy cried. "Grandma has a big wart on her leg!"
"Eat around it," his mother says.

"Mommy! Mommy! Can I lick the bowl?"

"Yes, but flush it first."

An old woman takes her elderly husband for his annual check-up. A nurse comes into the waiting room and says, "Before the doctor can see you, I'll need a stool sample and a urine sample."

The old man is hard of hearing. He says to his wife, "What did she say?"

The wife replies, "She says she needs to see a pair of your underpants."

President Clinton is in a top secret meeting with the heads of the CIA and the FBI. Suddenly, the head of the CIA shakes his head and sticks his finger in his ear.

"What are you doing?" Clinton asks.

"Well, Mr. President," the CIA chief says, "I have a receiver in my skull and a transmitter in my ear. I got a message and I was transmitting my reply."

A few minutes later, the FBI chief taps his front teeth and sticks his finger up his nose.

"And what are you doing?" Clinton asks the FBI chief.

"Well, Mr. President," the FBI guy replies, "I have a receiver planted in my front tooth and a transmitter in my nostril. I received a message and was transmitting my reply."

Five minutes later, Clinton stands up and blows a huge fart.

The FBI chief asks, "What are you doing, Mr. President?"

Clinton farts again and says, "I'm receiving a fax."

Did you hear about the blind skunk?

He had a long conversation with a fart.

———

Ida and Sheila meet on the street. Ida says to her friend, "So, Sheila, how are your children?"

Sheila says proudly, "Steven is a dentist and has a beautiful wife and three beautiful children. They have a big house in Long Island and a condo in Florida."

"And how's your other son, the one who's mentally retarded?" Ida asks.

Sheila says, "He's a lawyer."

What do you call a girl who farts all the time?

Fanny.

What do you call a girl who wets her bed every night?

Sissy.

What's green and carries a doctor's bag?

Mucous Welby

Why do women have legs?

So they won't leave snail tracks on the floor.

———

Man goes to the doctor and says, "Doc, you gotta help me. I've lost my memory."

The doctor tries to calm him down and says, "When did this happen?"

"When did what happen?" the patient asks.

———

What's more disgusting than a bathroom in the New York City subway?

The bathroom at a Bulemics Anonymous meeting.

The husband says to his wife, "Tomorrow is our thirtieth anniversary. How do you want to celebrate?"

The wife says, "I want to go somewhere I've never been before."

The husband replies, "Try the kitchen."

Why shouldn't you drink and drive?

You might hit a bump and spill your drink.

What's a Yuppie cannibal?

Someone who eats three squares a day.

How does a bulemic feed her cat?

She throws up in his dish.

What do you call a man with no arms and no legs, who likes to water ski?

Skip.

What's the definition of children?

Rotten little brats who live in your house and don't pay rent.

What's black and white and has a dirty name?

Sister Fuckface.

———

How can you tell when a Hell's Angel is happy?

He's got bugs in his teeth.

———

What do you call a girl who just got run over by an eighteen-wheeler?

Patty.

What do you call a girl with no arms and no legs, who lives in a cash register?

Penny.

What's the difference between a black and a Pakistani?

Five more minutes in the oven.

How many doctors does it take to screw in a lightbulb?

Depends on whether the bulb has health insurance.

What's the definition of a multicultural politician?

Someone who prefers to screw blacks and Hispanics.

———

What do you call a great artist with an attitude problem?

Vincent Van Go Fuck Yourself.

———

What does an elephant do with his back legs?

Haul ass.

Why can't lepers get a driver's license?

They always leave their feet on the gas.

GROSS GAY AND LESBIAN JOKES

What do you call one hundred fags and a Jew?

A musical.

What did the lesbian frog say to the other lesbian frog after they had sex?

"We really do taste like chicken!"

How do you punish a faggot?

Put Super Glue in his K Y Jelly.

What is AIDS?

A disease that makes vegetables out of fruits.

———

What do you call a fag with a hard-on?

A can opener.

———

Why do faggots want to join the Navy?

Because the Navy makes men.

How do you know when your doctor is gay?

He grabs your shoulders when he sticks the thermometer up your ass.

———

How do you kill a queer?

Homo-cide.

———

How did everyone know the bodybuilder was gay?

He got caught pumping Myron.

Why did the gay poker game turn into an orgy?

The queens were wild.

———

A woman gets on an elevator. Two queers are having a discussion.

The woman asks, "Going down?"

"We're still talking," says one of the queers.

A GROSS VARIETY

What is a Mexican vacation?

Cockroach races in the Wal-Mart parking lot.

Why do nuns masturbate?

Because the Lord helps those who help themselves.

Who do you get into a gay whorehouse?

You go through the back door.

Why do paranoid schizophrenics hate shaving?

They don't trust the son of a bitch holding the razor.

How can you tell when a twelve-year-old girl is having sex?

She has birth control pills shaped like Fred Flintstone.

Why is Jesus Christ horny?

He hasn't come in 2,000 years.

Why is rape so difficult?

Because a woman can run faster with her dress up than a guy can with his pants down.

———

How can you tell a prosperous Polack?

His garbage cans are equipped with burglar alarms.

———

How did the blind man get his arm ripped off?

He tried to read a speed limit sign that said "65 mph."

What did the barber say to the Italian kid?

"Haircut or oil change?"

———

How did the homosexual know he only had six weeks left to live?

A gerbil came out of his asshole and saw his shadow.

———

Thought for the day:

If a middle-aged ex-football hero had to go berserk and slaughter his wife, why couldn't it have been Frank Gifford?

What's the difference between a straight chick and a lesbian?

A straight chick loves a hard prick; a lesbian loves the box it comes in.

What flavor ice cream do lesbians like?

Catfish-mint.

How many Michael Jacksons does it take to screw in a lightbulb?

None. Michael Jackson only screws little boys.

What's the scariest part of being tried in a court of law?

The jury of twelve people too stupid to get out of jury duty.

———

Where do people shop in Alabama?

KKK-Mart.

Tyrone goes to see his buddy Julio at the hospital. Both of Julio's arms and one of his legs are in casts, both his eyes are black, and he has a big bandage wrapped around his head.

"Shit," Tyrone says. "What happened to you?"

"You know that gorgeous babe across the street, name of Mona?" Julio asks. "I was banging her brains out when her construction worker old man came home early."

"That's too bad," Tyrone says "But it could have been worse."

"Yeah?" Julio asks. "How?"

"If her husband came home an hour earlier," Tyrone replies, "he woulda beat the shit outta *me.*"

A Polack goes to a bar and says to the bartender, "Better make mine a double. I just saw my wife and my best friend get into my car and run off together for parts unknown."

"That's a tough break, mister," the bartender says sympathetically.

"You're telling me," the Polack replies. "I just bought that car."

———

A blind man walks into a department store and starts knocking stuff off the shelves, onto the floor.

"May I help you?" a clerk asks him.

"No thanks," the blind man says. "Just looking."

———

How do you know when your high school is really tough?

The school paper has an obituary page.

"My wife and I were happy for 25 years," Al tells his friend. "Then it all went straight down the toilet."

"What happened?"

"We met."

———

Guy says to his wife, "How come you never tell me when you're having an orgasm?"

Wife says, "Because you're never around when I do."

———

How did the faggot get AIDS from the toilet seat?

He sat on it before the last guy got up.

Why didn't the fag know who gave him AIDS?

Because he didn't have eyes in the back of his head.

———

Why did Adolf Hitler go broke?

He got his gas bill.

———

Why can't fags get auto insurance?

They get rear-ended too much.

What's the definition of a daredevil?

Someone who runs through Ethiopia with a sandwich around his neck.

———

What do you call a faggot from the South?

A homosex-y'all.

———

What's brown and hangs out in the forest?

Winnie's Pooh.

What's cold and stiff and wants to hold your hand?

John Lennon.

What's red and silver and walks into walls?

A baby with forks in his eyes.

What smells terrible and screams a lot?

A baby chewing on an electrical cord.

What do a tornado, a hurricane, and an Alabama divorce have in common?

Sooner or later, someone is going to lose their mobile home.

A female turtle is sexually assaulted by three snails on her way home. She calls the cops. When they arrive, they begin to question her.

"Did you see the assailants?" one cop asks the lady turtle.

"No," she replies.

The cop says, "Miss, if you didn't see your attackers, I don't know if we can help you."

"You have to understand," the lady turtle says. "It all happened so fast!"

What's the difference between a whale and a lesbian?

Fifty pounds and a flannel shirt.

———

So the redneck goes to pick up his date, a very respectable girl from a good home on the other side of the tracks. As she got ready, her mother waited upstairs, then heard a strange sound coming from the hallway.

The mother calls down to the redneck, "Excuse me, young man, but are you spitting in the vase?"

"No, ma'am," the redneck replies. "But I'm gettin' closer each time."

What do you get when you cross a nun with a serial killer?

A twisted sister.

What do you call a Polish boomerang?

A stick.

What is Polish diarrhea?

A brain drain.

Three construction workers—one Jewish, one Italian, and one Polish—are sitting on the fiftieth floor girder. It's lunchtime.

The Jew opens his lunchbox and says in disgust, "Oy, salami again! Every day my wife Sophie gives me salami. This is the last time. If she gives me salami tomorrow, I'm jumping off this building!"

The Italian opens his lunchbox. "Again a hero sandwich," he complains. Every day my Maria gives me a hero sandwich. This is the last time. If she gives me a hero sandwich tomorrow, I'm also jumping off this building!"

The Polack opens his lunchbox and says, "Kielbasa again! This is the last time. If I get kielbasa tomorrow, I'm going to jump off this building, too!"

The next day, the Jew opens his lunchbox. Sure enough, it's a salami sandwich. The Jew jumps off the girder and falls fifty floors to the street. The Italian opens his lunchbox. Sure enough, there sits a hero sandwich. He screams and hurls himself off the building after the Jew.

The Polack opens his lunchbox. Inside is kielbasa. He likewise jumps off the building.

As he's falling to the street and certain death, the Polack says, "What the hell am I doing? I always pack my own lunch!"

THAT'S NOT FUNNY, THAT'S SICK!

What's red, white, fat, and falls down chimneys?

Santa Klutz

Why is the Roman Catholic Church finally letting priests marry?

So they'll know what hell *really* is.

Why don't Italians take showers?

Because oil and water don't mix.

A man walks into a whorehouse and gives the madam five hundred dollars. He says to her, "Give me the fattest, ugliest, most rotten-tempered whore you have."

"For five hundred dollars," says the madam, "you can have the very best."

"You don't understand," the man says. "I'm not horny. I'm just homesick."

Why do penises have heads on them?

So your hand doesn't slide off.

How does an old man keep his youth?

He gives her lots of money.

A man is at the gates of Heaven waiting to get in. St. Peter says to him, "Not so fast, mister. You don't get into Heaven that easy. Have you done something truly wonderful in your life that would qualify you to get into Heaven?"

The man replies, "Well, I was a member of the Mafia until I testified against the godfather in Federal Court and helped him get sentenced to fifty years to life."

St. Peter says, "That's great. When did this happen?"

The man replies, "About ten minutes ago."

How do you know when your wife is frigid?

When she opens her legs, the refrigerator light goes on.

How does a yuppie chick know when she's having an orgasm?

She drops her briefcase.

Al decides to stop for a quick beer at his local bar on his way home from work. Just as he's getting ready to leave, however, he meets a gorgeous blonde. They start talking, and pretty soon she invites him back to her apartment.

Before long, they end up in bed, and go at it most of the night. After their fifth time, Al looks up at the clock. It's almost six in the morning.

He leaps out of bed and grabs the phone, and starts dialing. When his wife answers—sounding angry—Al blurts out, "Don't pay the ransom, honey. I just escaped!"

The teacher at P.S. 129 in New York City was teaching her third grade class about farm animals.

She asks the Italian kid, "Mario, what does a chicken sound like?"

Mario replies, "The chicken, he go *cluck, cluck, cluck.*"

"That's correct," the teacher says. To an Irish kid, she asks, "Patrick, what does a cow sound like?"

Patrick answers, "The cow goes *moooo.*"

"Correct," responds the teacher. To the black kid, she asks, "Tyrone, what does a pig sound like?"

Tyrone shouts, *'Freeze, motherfucker!"*

What's the definition of a black mermaid?

A catfish with big tits.

What time was the funeral for the movie theater owner?

1:30, 3:30, 5:30, 7:30 and 9:30.

How do you know when a guy is really cheap?

When he dies, he gets buried in a rented tuxedo.

What happens when you eat in a Chinese-German restaurant?

An hour later, you're hungry for power.

You know you just married a German girl when . . .

1. Her monocle falls off during the ceremony.
2. Her family signs the guest book, then burns it.
3. You can't keep your new father-in-law away from the machine gun.

Why do alligators make the smartest parents?

They eat their young.

How can you tell when there's a Polack at a cockfight?

He enters a parrot.

How can you tell when there's a black guy at a cockfight?

He bets on the parrot.

How can you tell when there's an Italian at a cockfight?

The parrot wins.

What does a black parrot say?

"Polly want a white bitch."

A man walks into a restaurant that guarantees any dish cooked to order, or you don't pay.

The man says to the waiter, "I want a plate of steaming shit."

The waiter can't believe his ears. He says, "That's impossible, sir. This is a four-star restaurant."

The customer replies, "Your sign out there says any dish cooked to order or I don't pay. If you refuse to cook me a plate of steaming shit, I'll sue you for a million dollars."

The waiter goes off and relays the order to the chef. Knowing they have no choice, the waiter and the chef each take a big dump on a plate. The waiter goes off to deliver the order to the customer. Two minutes later he's back, covered with shit from head to toe.

"What happened? the cook asks.

The waiter says, "He said he wouldn't eat the shit because there was a hair in it."

Why do dobermans lick their asses?

To get the taste of niggers out of their mouths.

A woman goes to see her gynecologist. He puts her into the stirrups, then begins to examine her.

"My God . . . my God," the gynecologist says. "This is the biggest pussy I've ever seen . . . the biggest pussy I've ever seen."

"I know," says the woman, "but you don't have to say it twice."

"I didn't," says the gynecologist.

What is Michael Jackson's favorite movie?

Close Encounters of the Third Grade.

What's stupid and says, "Life is like a box of chocolate laxatives?"

Forrest Dump.

What's the definition of Jello?

Kool-Aid with a hard-on.

What do you get when you cross Sylvester Stallone and Dolly Parton?

Rocky Mountains.

———

How can you spot a horny nun?

She's the one with the vibrating crucifix.

———

What's one page long and full of lies?

The Polish Book of World Records.

———

Why are black women such good dishwashers?

Because the Brillo pad is built right in.

Why did God create women?

Because sheep won't do windows.

———

What do you call a constipated Chinaman?

Hung Chow.

———

How does a Jewish girl define sex?

Two minutes of pleasure and two hours of guilt.

A man goes to see his urologist, who informs him that he'll need a sperm sample.

Two gorgeous nurses take the man into an examination room. There, they proceed to undress him, then undress themselves. They seduce the guy, getting him all aroused, then go down on him until he comes, and they get their sperm sample.

Returning to the waiting room, the happy patient opens the wrong door. Inside a small room are two black guys jerking off over copies of *Hustler.*

The patient asks the urologist, "What's with those guys?"

The urologist responds, "Oh, they're on welfare."

What is the definition of gross?

Dreaming you're eating chocolate pudding and waking up with a spoon in your asshole.

What did one gerbil say to the other gerbil?

"Let's go down to Greenwich Village and get shitfaced."

———

What has big lips and falls off the Empire State Building?

Martin Luther King Kong, Jr.

———

How do you know when you're getting old?

When they ask to check your bags and you don't have any.

The mayor is running for reelection. He tells his loyal constituents, "Yesterday, I rented an X-rated video cassette, and you won't believe what I saw: three acts of oral sex, four acts of anal sex, a woman making it with a dog, and another woman servicing five men. If I'm elected, I promise to rid our community of these vulgar videos. Are there any questions?"

A man in the back of the room asks, "Yes. Where did you rent that tape?"

———

What's Michael Jackson's favorite expression?

"Spare the rod, spoil the child."

———

What's a Jewish nymphomaniac?

A woman who lets her husband make love to her *after* she's had her hair done.

What's the difference between a stud and a premature ejaculator?

One's good for seconds, the other's also good for seconds.

What does a sheep herder do when he gets bored?

He buries himself in his work.

What's the difference between a fox and a pig?

About half a dozen beers.

What's the difference between a Arab and a bucket of shit?

The bucket.

Why did the Polish kid have twelve pairs of underwear?

One for each month.

What do tits and model train sets have in common?

They're both for little kids, but daddy plays with them, too.

What's the favorite game show in Alabama?

"Maim that Coon."

What do you call a black hitchhiker?

Stranded.

How do gay men have a fight?

They exchange blows.

What do women use to clean their twats in India?

Bangla-douche.

What do you call an Italian pool player?

Minestrone Fats

The Jewish woman turns to her husband early one morning and says, "Arnold, I just dreamed you bought me a mink coat."

"Fine," Arnold replies. "Tomorrow night when you dream, wear it in good health."

What's blue and comes in brownies?

Cub Scouts.

———

What does a proctologist do when his patient wants a second opinion?

He uses two fingers.

———

What's the difference between a porcupine and the White House?

A porcupine has its pricks on the outside.

———

What happens when a Polack stops paying his garbage bill?

They stop delivering.

What's gay and comes in washing machines?

The May-fag Man.

———

What do you get when you cross Arnold Schwarzenegger and a Jew?

Conan the Wholesaler.

———

Why do fags grow moustaches?

To hide the stretch marks.

How do you know when a guy is gay?

He tries to butter you up.

———

A gay guy is driving down the street, not paying attention. He smashes into the back of a delivery truck.

The truck driver, a muscular Brooklyn-type, gets out of his smashed truck and starts yelling at the homo.

"You dumb little bastard," the truck driver rants. "You drive like shit, and you can kiss my ass!"

"Thank God," the homo says. "You want to settle out of court!"

How do you know when you live in a Yuppie neighborhood?

The fire department uses Evian water.

———

Why is Italian bread so long?

So you can dip it in the sewer.

———

What's black, crispy, and sits on your roof?

An Italian electrician.

Why don't debutantes like orgies?

Too many thank-you notes to write.

Why do hunters make the best lovers?

Because they go deep into the bush, shoot more than once, and always eat what they shoot.

UNBEARABLY DISGUSTING

Why did God create man first?

Because he didn't want a woman around telling him what to do.

Why did the anorexic shoot her dog?

It kept trying to bury her.

What do you call ten black fags butt-fucking?

Soul Train

How do you know you've got a tiny pecker?

You put it in her hand and she says, "No thanks, I don't smoke."

How do you know when you're really old?

Your blood type is discontinued.

How can you tell when a ladder is designed for Polacks?

The word STOP is painted on the top rung.

How can you tell a secretary is Polish?

She's the one with White-Out all over her computer screen.

Hear about the female tuna fish?

She smelled like a Polish woman.

How did Dolly Parton get two black eyes?

She went jogging and forgot to wear a bra.

What's the latest fashion craze in Bosnia?

Body Bags by Gucci.

An elderly couple goes to the doctor for the annual check-up. The husband goes in first.

During the examination, the doctor says, "So, Harry, how's your sex life?"

"It's just fine, doc," the old man says. "The first time is great, but the second time we do it, I sweat like a pig."

"Second time?" the doctor asks, amazed. "Harry, you're 88 years old!"

Later, after Harry is gone and his 86-year-old wife comes in for her check-up, the doctor says, "Sophie, Harry and I were talking about your sex life. He said the first time is fine, but the second time, he starts to sweat."

"It's true," Sophie replies. "In January it's cold, and in August it's hot."

What was the sequel to *White Men Can't Jump?*

Black Men Never Shut the Fuck Up at the Movies

Hear about the Polish anti-abortion demonstration?

They picketed a coat-hanger factory.

What motto does a child molester live by?

"It's not how old you are, it's what age you feel."

———

What's the worst advice you can give to a black guy?

Be yourself.

———

How can you tell a bride at a Bosnian wedding?

She's the one laying next to the groom.

———

What's the definition of a schmuck?

Someone who gets out of the shower to take a leak.

What do you call people who circumcise whales?

Foreskin-divers.

Why do queers make lousy Santas?

Instead of filling your stocking, they want to try it on.

Two Italians are hanging out at the corner bar. Guido seems deeply depressed. His friend, Patsy, asks him, "What's the matter with you, Guido?"

Guido responds, "I'm having trouble with my mother-in-law."

"Everyone has trouble with their mother-in-law," Patsy says.

"Maybe," Guido tells his friend, "but not everyone gets her pregnant."

———

What do you get when you cross a WASP and a black man?

A fast abortion.

What's the best aspect of being bisexual?

You double your chances of getting a date on Saturday night.

———

A black man goes before the judge. The judge says to him, "You stand accused of robbing a convenience store and shooting the clerk six times. How do you plead?"

"Not guilty, your honor," the black man says.

"Are you saying you didn't do it?" the judge asks.

"No," the black guy replies. "I just didn't run fast enough."

Why do comedians have such lousy sex lives?

They perform for six minutes and women laugh at them.

———

How do you know when you haven't cleaned out your refrigerator in a long time?

You find a milk carton with a picture of the Lindberg baby on it.

———

How do you quit masturbating?

You go cold jerky.

How did the butcher get behind in his work?

He backed into the meat grinder.

———

Why were thermometers outlawed in Iran?

They caused brain damage.

———

What's the definition of being black balled?

An orgy at an NAACP meeting.

What's a racist's favorite soup?

Klan chowder.

———

How do black babies begin life?

As M&M-bryos.

———

What's black, seven feet tall, and cleans hotel rooms?

Wilt Chambermaid.

A big black guy walks into a bar and announces, "I got a twelve inch dick and I like to use it to fuck white women."

A drunk down at the end of the bar says, "I don't blame you, pal. I wouldn't fuck a nigger chick, either."

Why did the old Polish woman have her tubes tied?

She figured ten grandchildren were enough.

Why did the Jewish guy plant Cheerios in his garden?

He thought they were bagel seeds.

"You know," said one cannibal to his friend, "I really hate my mother-in-law."

"The hell with her," replies his friend. "Just eat the noodles."

———

A Polish teenager goes into a drugstore and says to the druggist, "How much are a package of condoms?"

The druggist replies, "$4.95, plus forty cents for tax."

"Aha," the Polish kid says. "I always wondered how you kept them on."

Adam and Eve make love for the first time. Afterwards, God comes to them and asks Adam, "Well, my son, did you enjoy having sex?"

Adam nods. "I liked it very much, it was great."

"And did Eve enjoy it?" God wants to know.

"Yes, she did," Adam replies. "She enjoyed it as much as I did."

"By the way, where is Eve?" God asks.

"She's down by the river, washing," Adam tells the Almighty.

Suddenly, God grows very angry. The skies darken, and God begins to swear.

"What's wrong?" Adam asks, cowering in fear.

"What's wrong?" God echoes "Eve is down washing in the river. Now I'll never get that smell out of the fish!"

Then there was the hooker who hung a sign on her door at noontime: "Gone to lunch. Go fuck yourself."

What do you call a Jewish-Mexican restaurant?

Casa Hadassah.

The husband and wife had been married for twenty years. Watching the news one evening, they saw a story about a man who swapped his wife for a season pass to the New York Knicks.

The wife asks her husband, "Darling, would you swap me for a season pass to the Knicks games?"

"Hell no," the husband replies. "The season's already half over.